For Klaus, danke für alles—J.W.

To Poppy and Lara—T.R.

American edition published in 2018 by Andersen Press USA, an imprint of Andersen Press Ltd., www.andersenpressusa.com
First published in Great Britain in 2018 by Andersen Press Ltd., 20 Vauxhall Bridge Road, London SW1V 2SA.

Distributed in the United States and Canada by Lerner Publishing Group, Inc.
241 First Avenue North Minneapolis, MN 55401 USA
For reading levels and more information, look up this title at www.lernerbooks.com.
Printed and bound in Malaysia by Tien Wah Press.
Library of Congress Cataloging-in-Publication Data Available
ISBN: 978-1-5415-3569-5
eBook ISBN: 978-1-5415-3570-1

1–TWP–6/1/18

Not Just a Book

Jeanne Willis

Tony Ross

ANDERSEN PRESS USA

This is not **just** a book.

You can use it as a hat . . .

. . . or a tent for your cat.

It can keep a table steady.

It can prop a floppy teddy.

You can use it as a funnel . . .

. . . or a toy train tunnel.

A brick for building towers . . .

. . . or a thing for pressing flowers.

1.
Put your flower here!
2.
Shut your book.
3. Stand on your book for a week!

A book is never just a book.

It can swat away a fly . . .

. . . hide your face if you are shy.

Shoo away a scary bear . . .

. . . and catch a fairy in midair.

Or keep the wasps out of your drink.

But
books
are
MORE
than
words
and
ink.
Not just a book

They can make you laugh

and weep.

And they can help you go to sleep.

Books can make you really clever . . .

. . . and they stay with you forever.
But the very best thing a book can do . . .

. . . is to be read and loved by YOU.